Life Is with People
by Atticus Lish

tyrant books

Copyright © 2011 Atticus Lish

All rights reserved

ISBN 978-0-9913608-5-7

Layout design by Ryan P. Kirby

www.nytyrant.com

Introduction

My primary goal in producing this book is to meet people with similar interests. It is my way of reaching out. Meeting people is so hard. It will be obvious that the book is mainly drawn from life, though there is an element of wish-fulfillment — not everything you see is real. Some material is imagined. Susan Sontag and HBO Asia were both sources of inspiration. I am a romantic. I hope that you will not disdain a work that is the product of a romantic imagination. Today's books are usually formulas for winning at sports or business, but what about friendship — or even something more intimate? The intimacy of the hitchhiker and the J.B. Hunt driver who gives him a lift? No one talks about that, especially in academia. This book ventures to fill that void. It is also a story of a coming-of-age (bildungsroman). And a cautionary tale whose point is clear. Its point is that I would like to have some time with you.

AL

It's hard to look at, I know.

You have to buy into it a little

to make it work,

the same as anything.

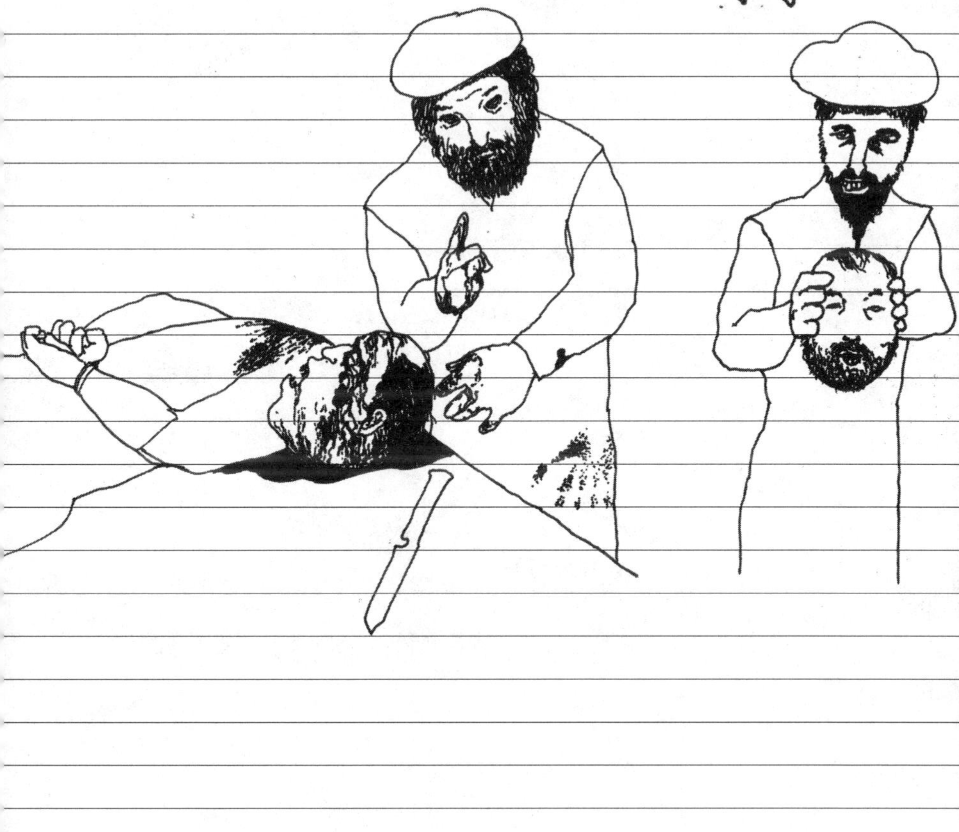

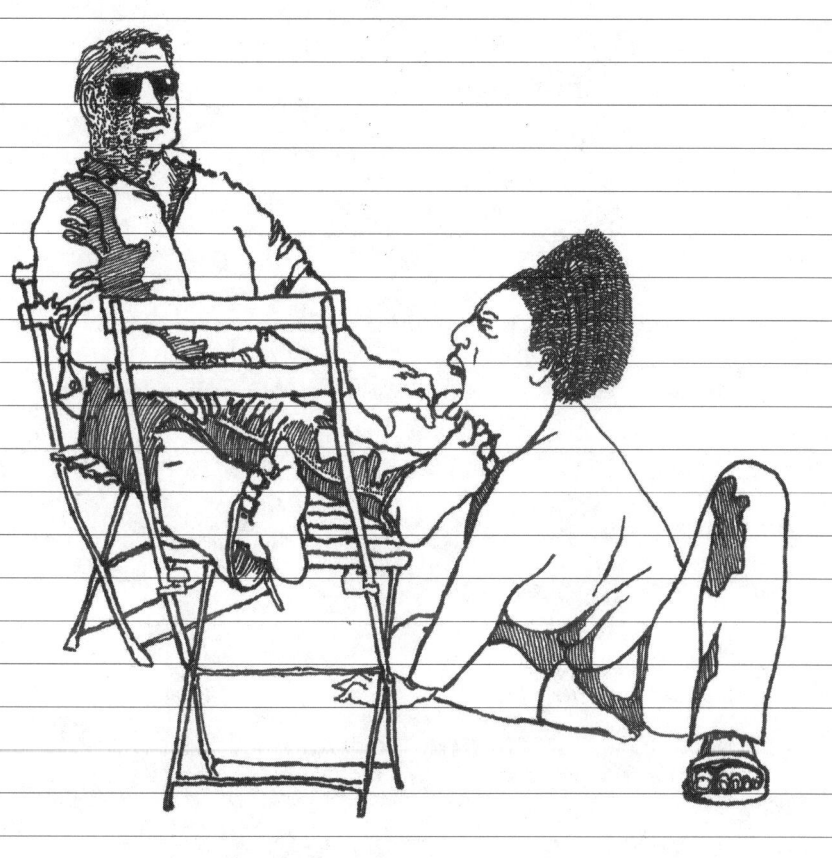

The Euro has never been stronger.

Even though Bernie was not housebroken, Yorgi kept him around because he was a whiz at portfolio management.

As parents, Mr. and Mrs. Krapowski did everything they could to protect their children from the horrors of the world.

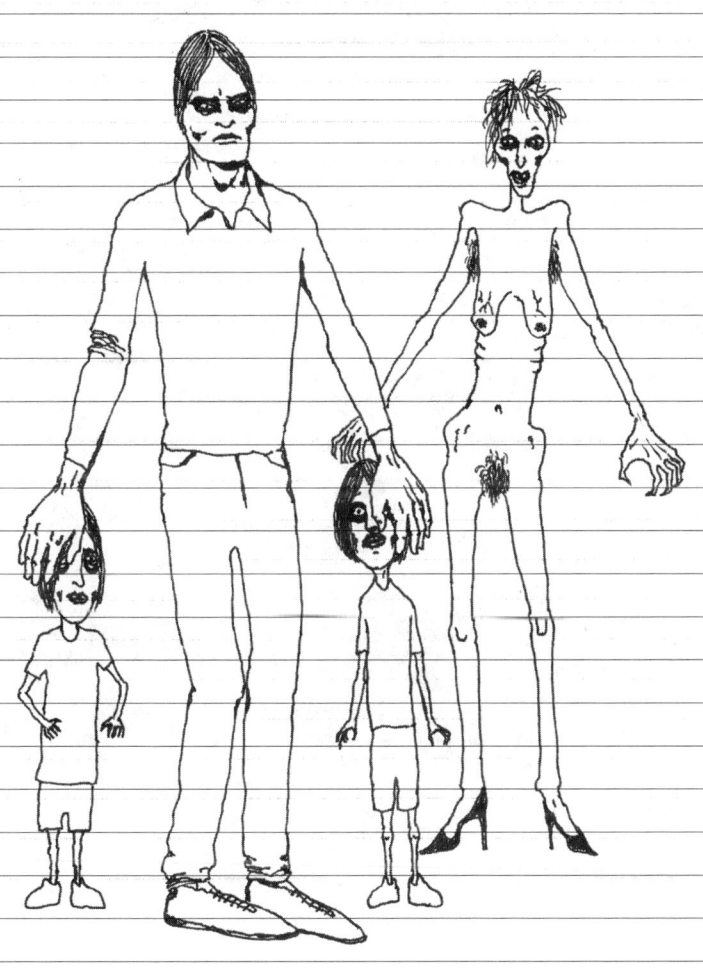

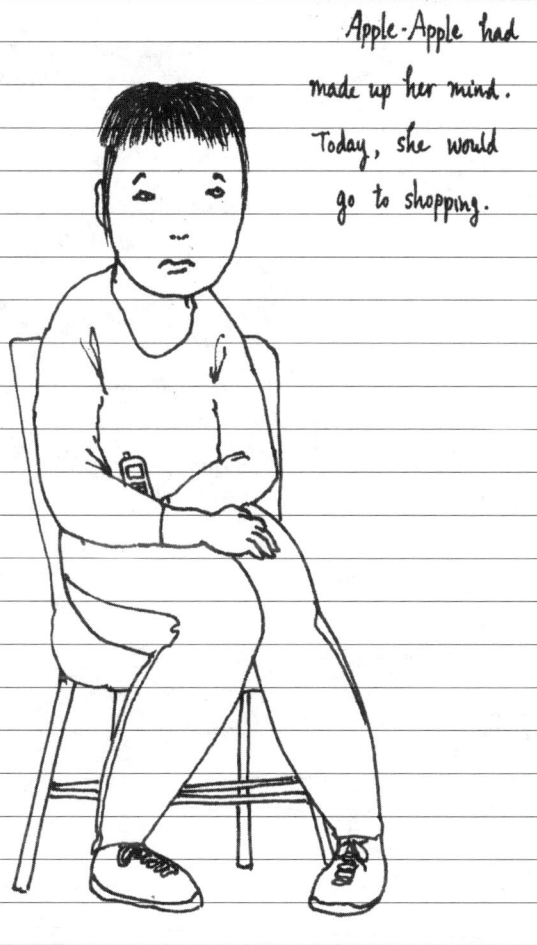

Chances were he would never be the same again.

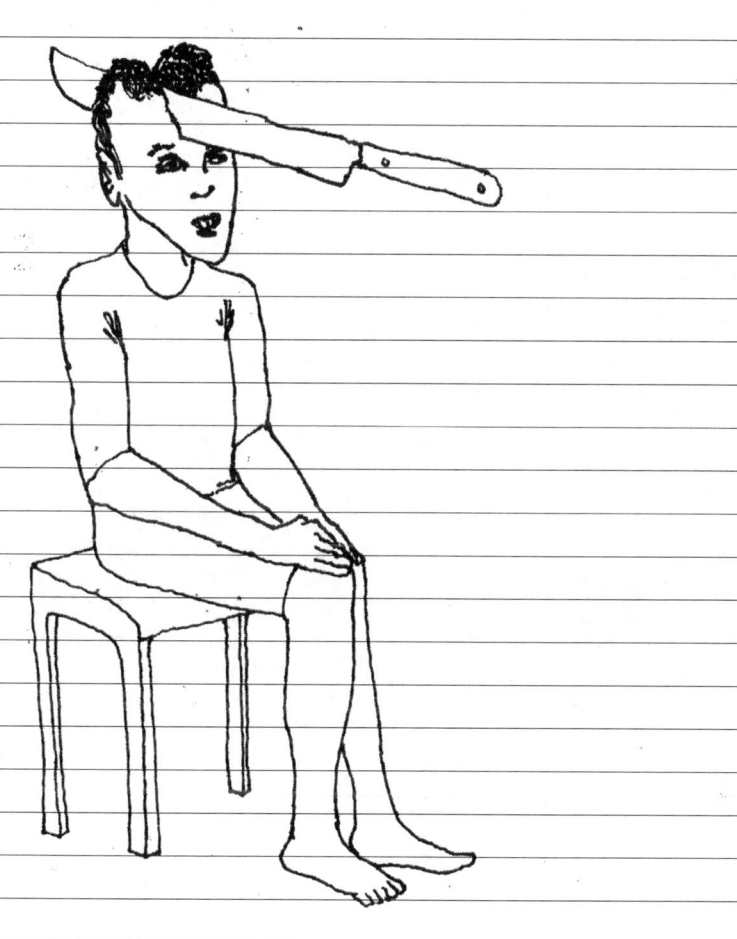

First you eats you food, then you plays with you ball and you friends.

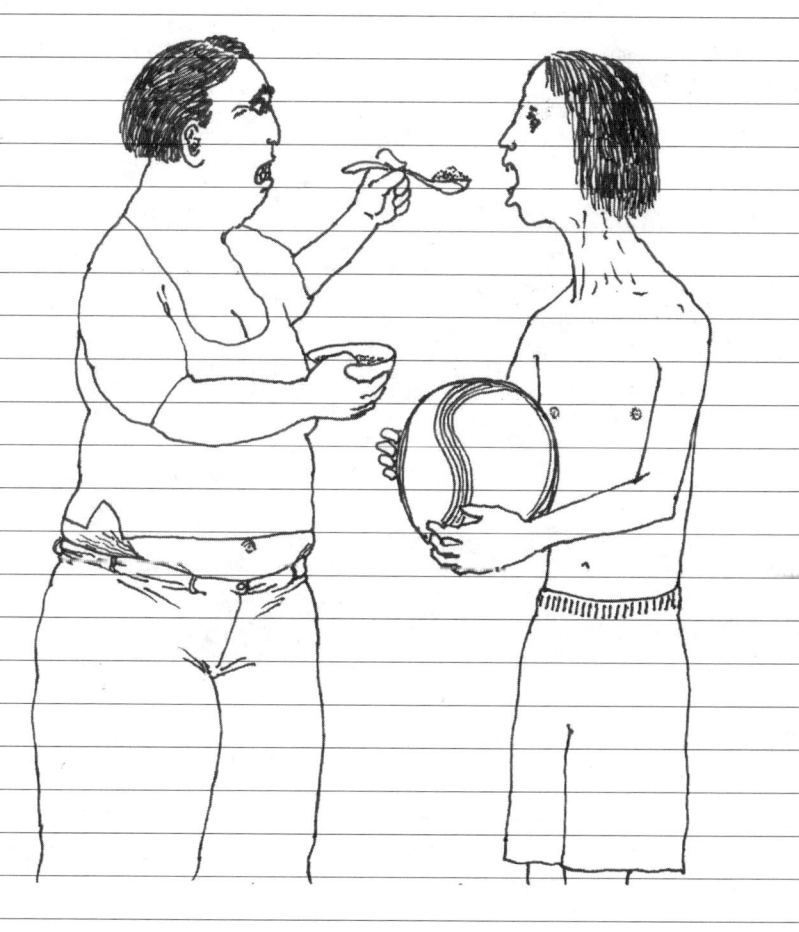

Apache and captured Dyker Heights youth

Anything that gets me out of the Bat Mitzvah.

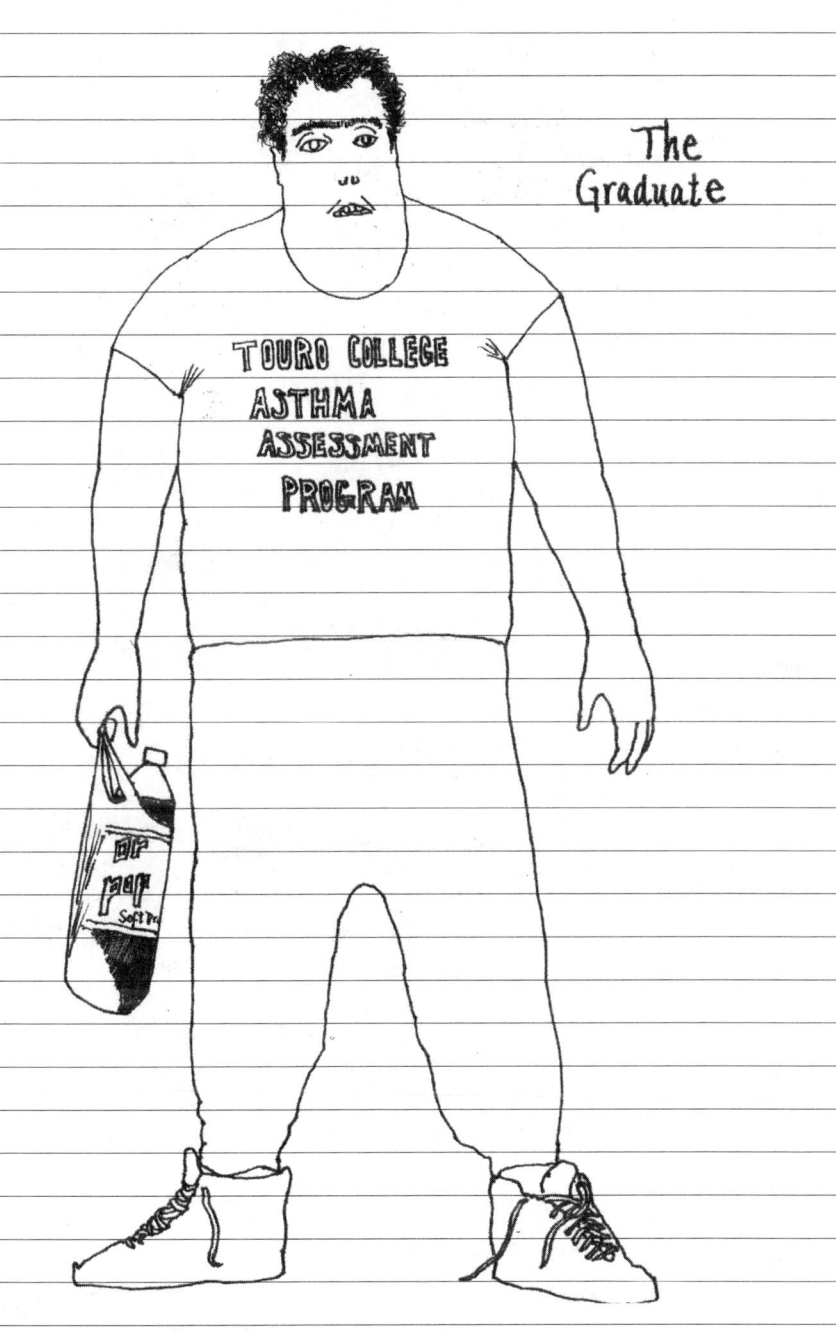

Same great friendship, awesome new handshake!

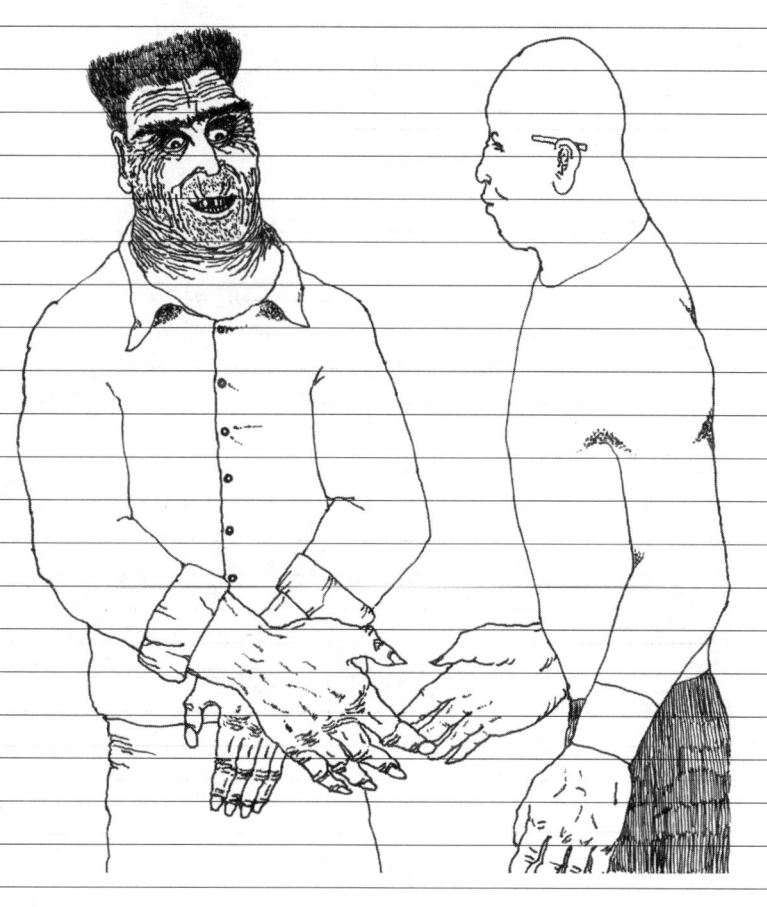

Making cupcakes — on my terms.

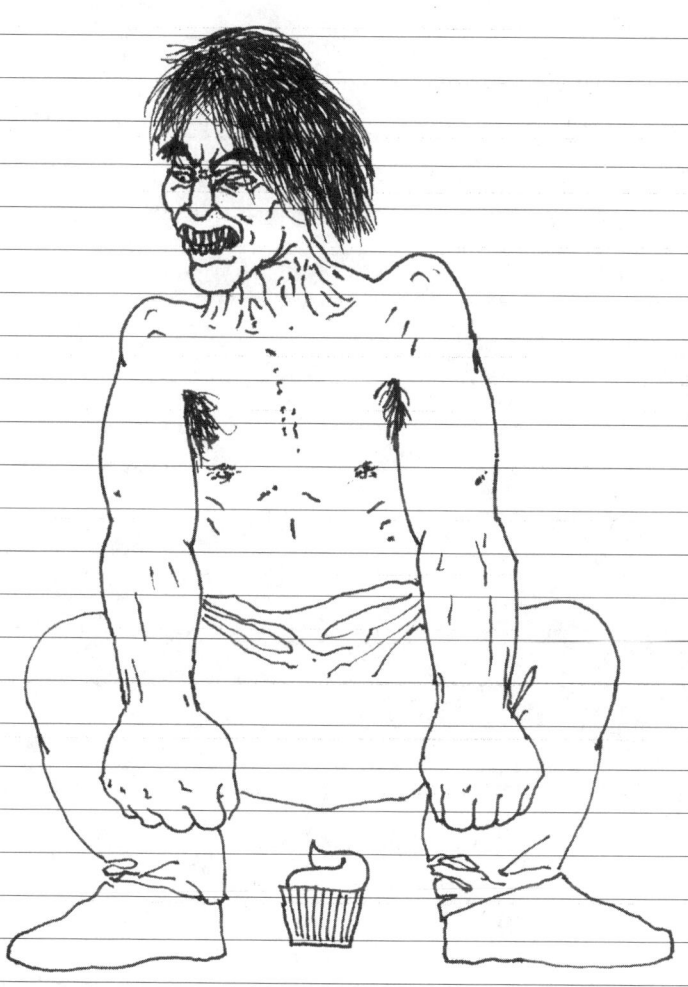

Man, I don't know what it is about this fuckin bunny? I just feel like I have to study it and learn from it all the time. And I feel like it knows what it's doin to me too.

Macedonian woman practicing the "jumping splits".

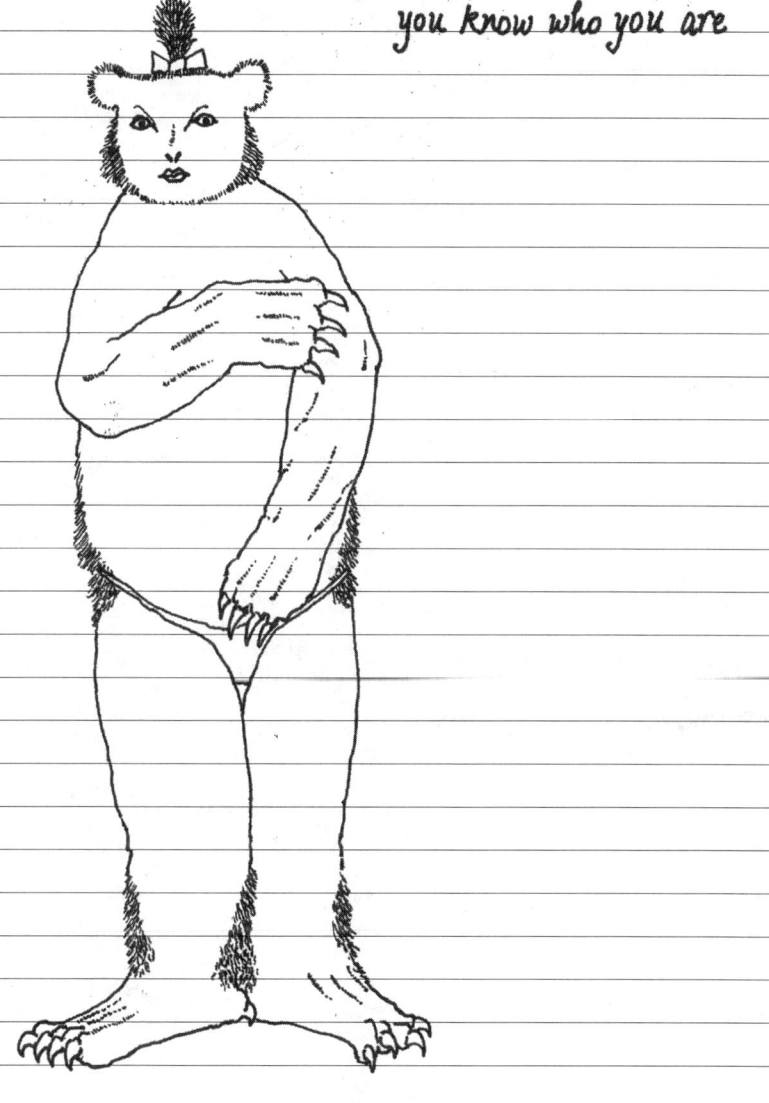

You to seem to react so negatively to me. That's all I know. And it hurts... it hurts.

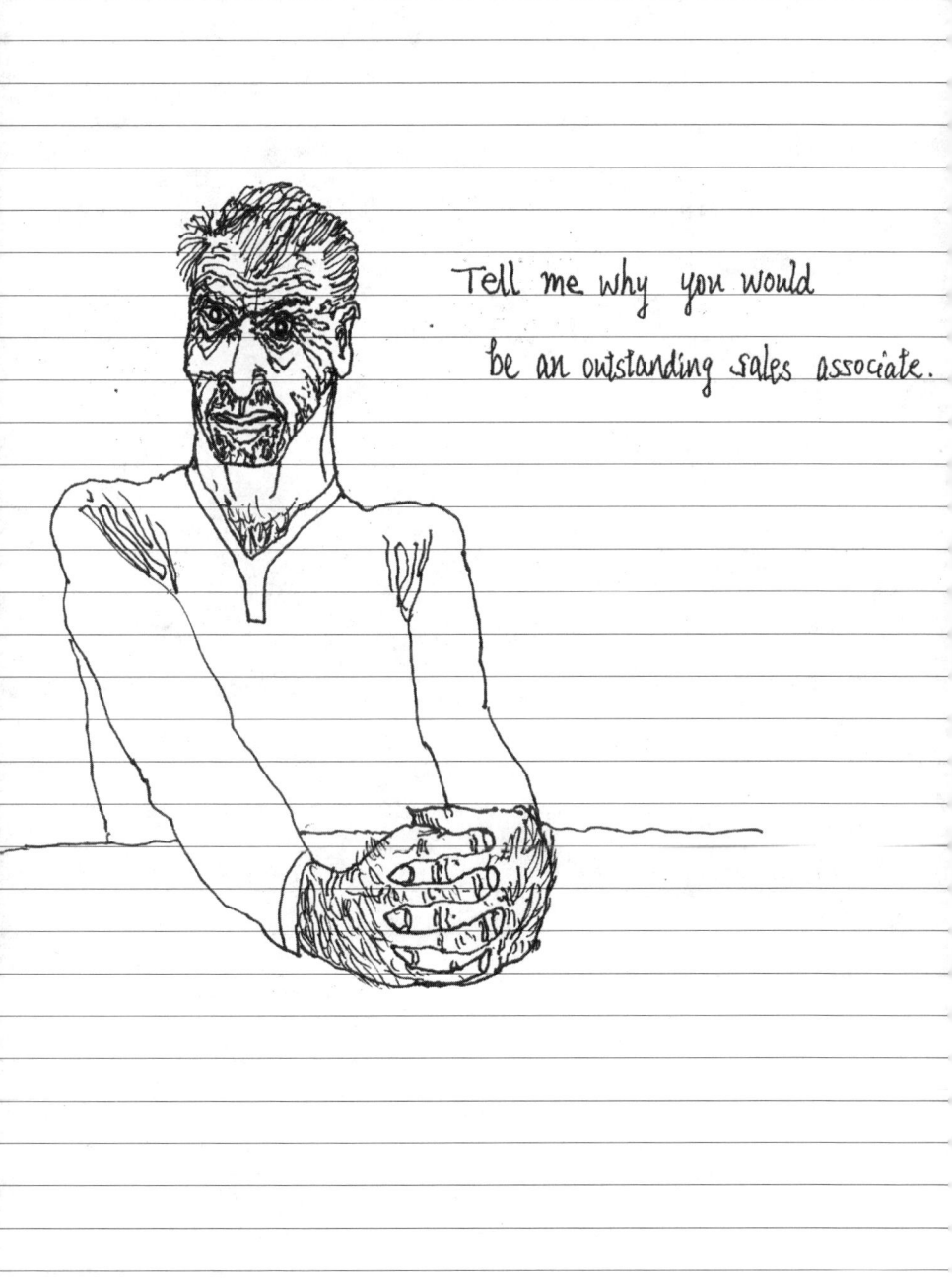

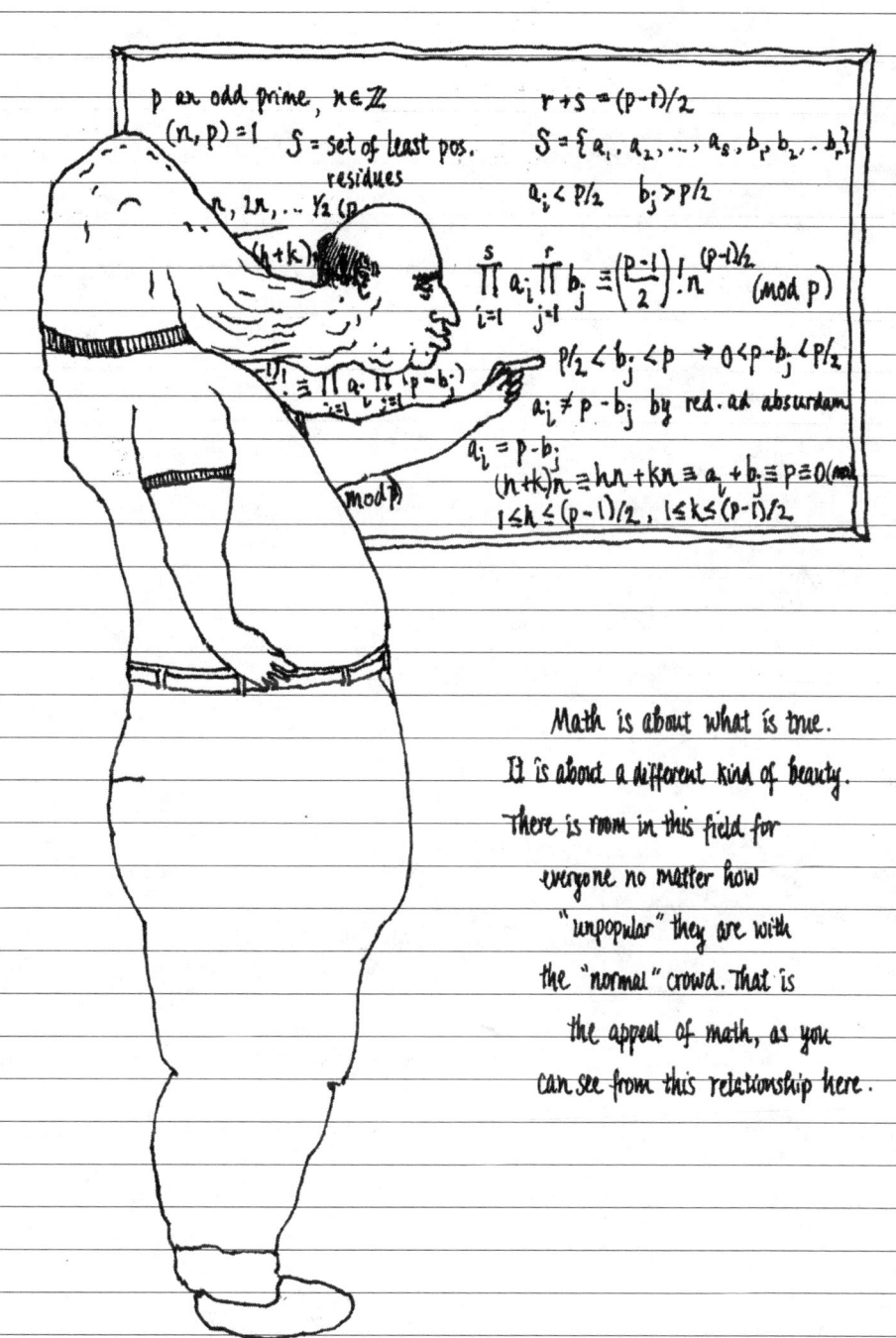

Math is about what is true. It is about a different kind of beauty. There is room in this field for everyone no matter how "unpopular" they are with the "normal" crowd. That is the appeal of math, as you can see from this relationship here.

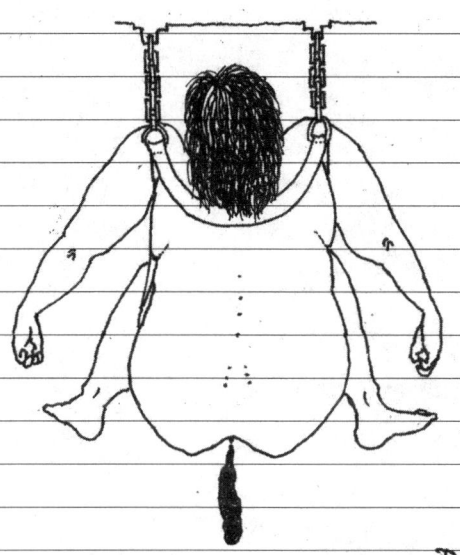

Boy meets girl, girl shits on boy's face — it was a fairytale right out of the Village Voice.

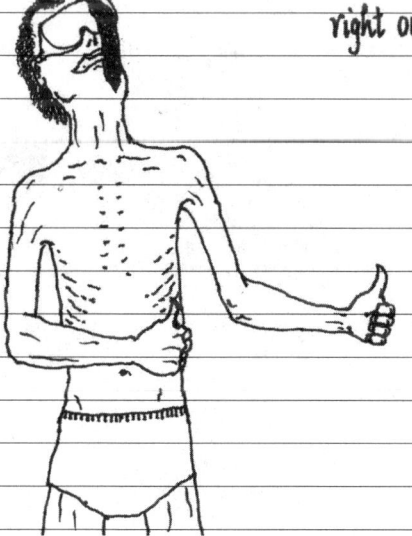

Flossing ~ an art as well as a science.

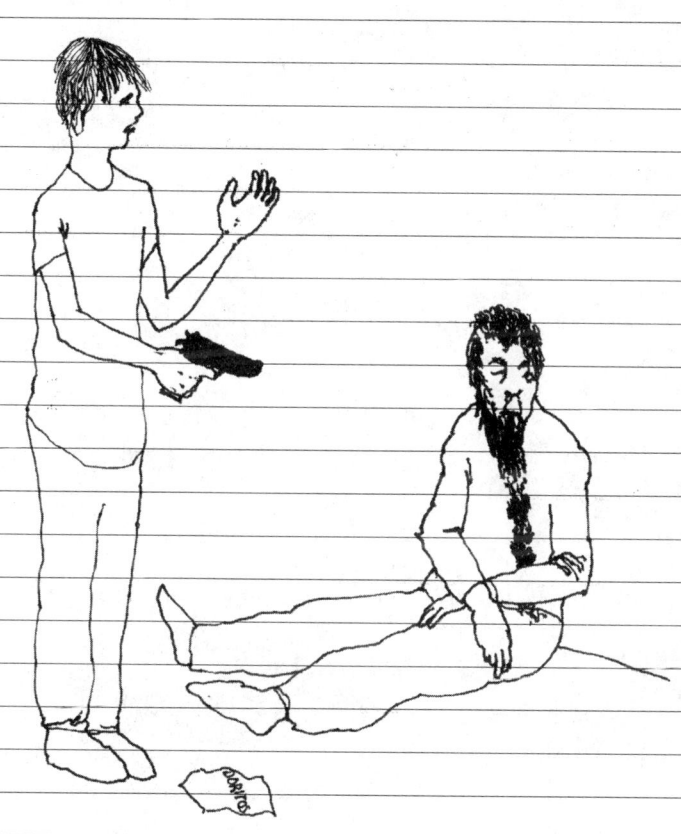

Nothing had prepared Edwin for the severity of the food cravings that followed killing.

Everything changes, but shopping at the Associated in Marine Park — that was still the same.

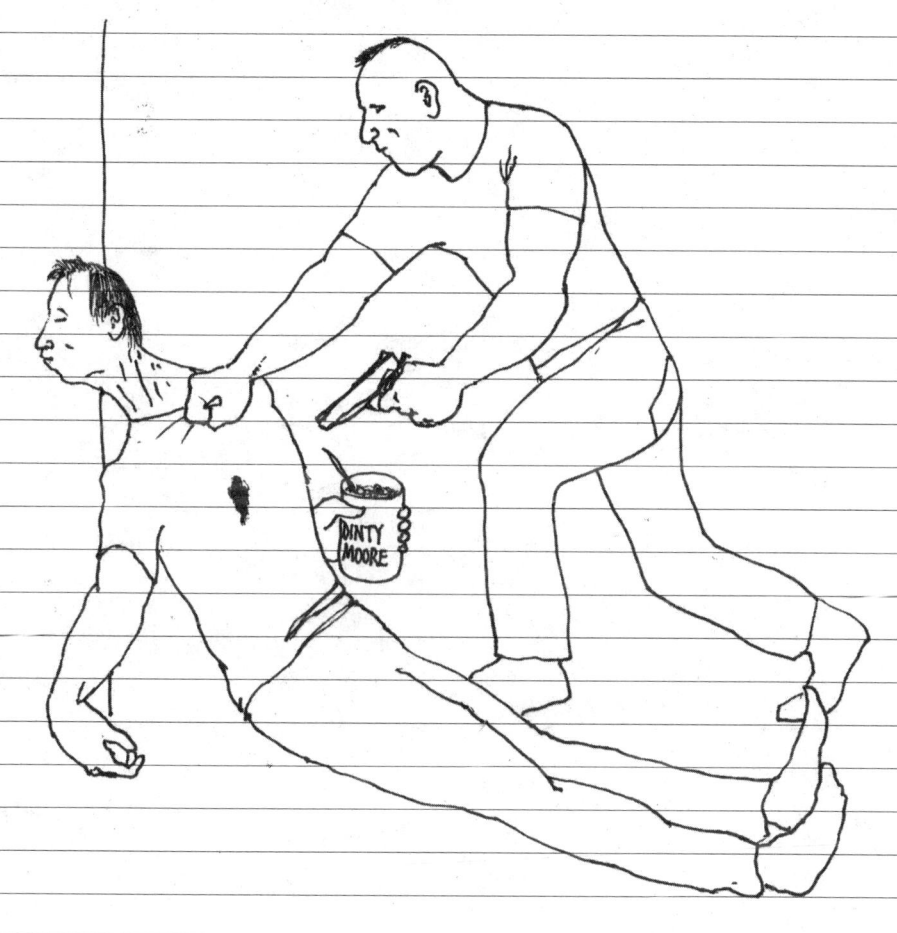

Do you accept Tony Danza in your heart?

Yes!

Tony! Come and get it!

Tell me at once where Mr. Danza is hiding... or I will tear this place apart.

It thrilled Julian to think that, years from now, after he and the beautiful stranger were celebrating their silver wedding anniversary, they would look back and smile remembering the night they met behind the Autozone.

Something told Kiki that she and Koko belonged together.

It has been a long day. Since 4 o'clock this morning, Ernie has been attempting to read and emotionally comprehend Dietz's classic work on retaining wall construction — with perhaps predictable results.

I don't secretly hate you. I hate you openly.

When they asked her why she had done it (as she knew they would), she resolved that she would tell them everything, from the early years of tender romance to the type of man he had become, so different in private from the public image: how he had made her abase herself.

Our relationship has improved a lot since we started doing more things together. Now we're eating a lot of the same foods. She reads with me. If there's a part she wants me to reread, she like underlines it with her tongue. That's what tells me to read it again. I've even noticed Linda getting jealous — and she should, man. It's justified.

There's nothing wrong with me, darlin'.

On the horns of my first major dilemma.

"Must lie perfectly still..."

"Ooooo"

Leg lift: still got the old razzle-dazzle!

It's just indigestion... or is it?

The evening was a complete success except for a minor hiccup caused by Frank's "intestinal issue."

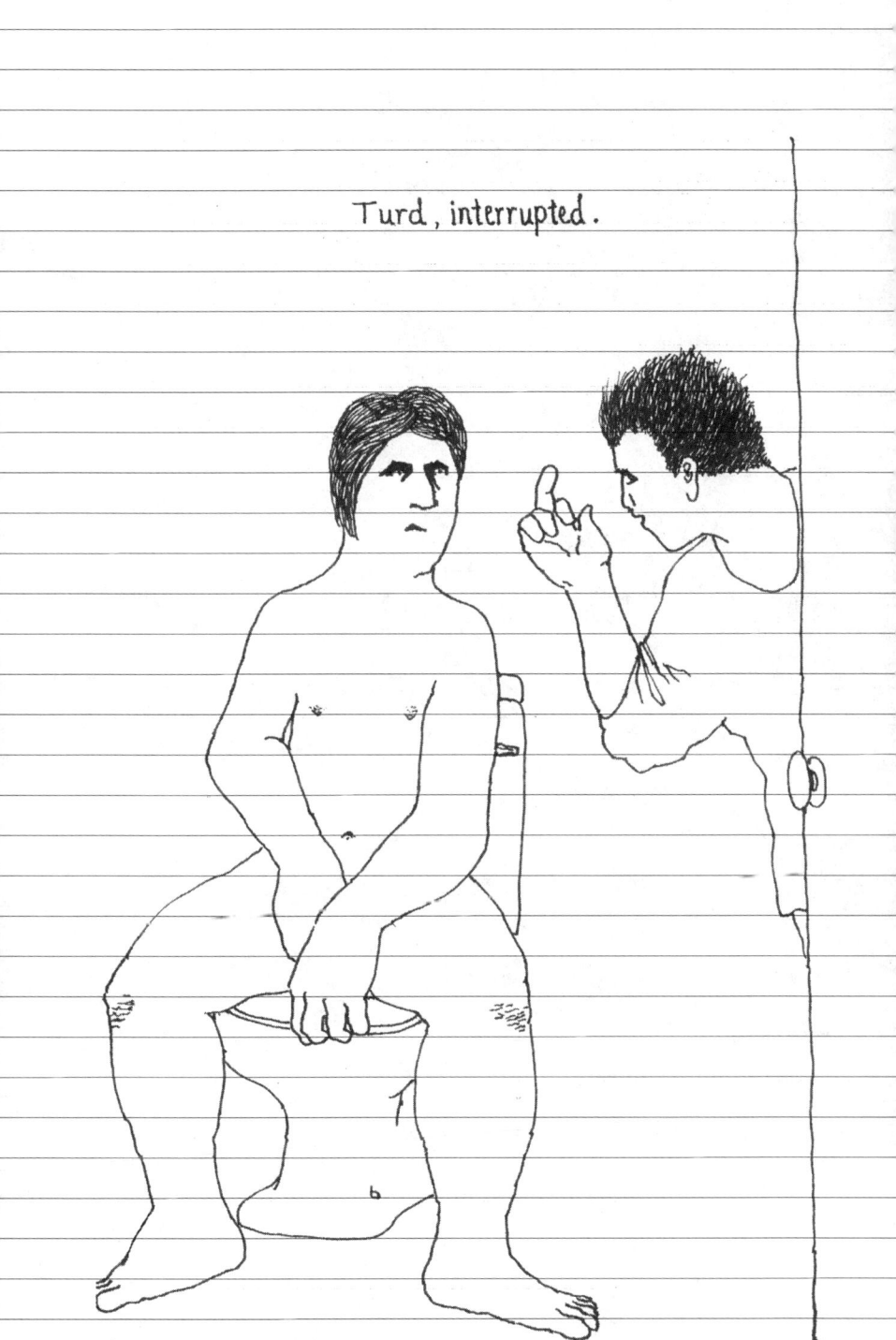

Almighty washes hands with soap and hot water before going back to work, just like it says in the Torah.

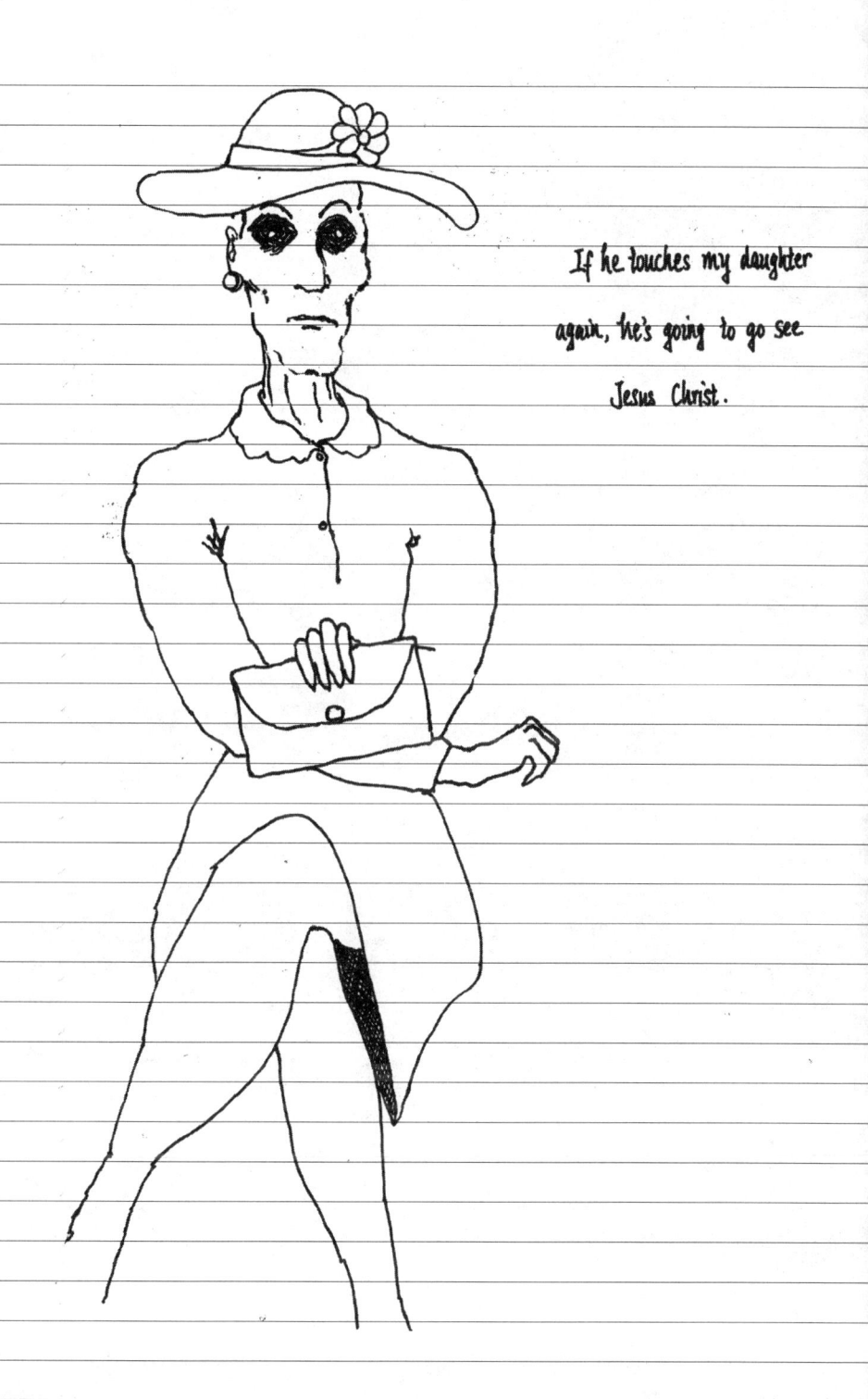

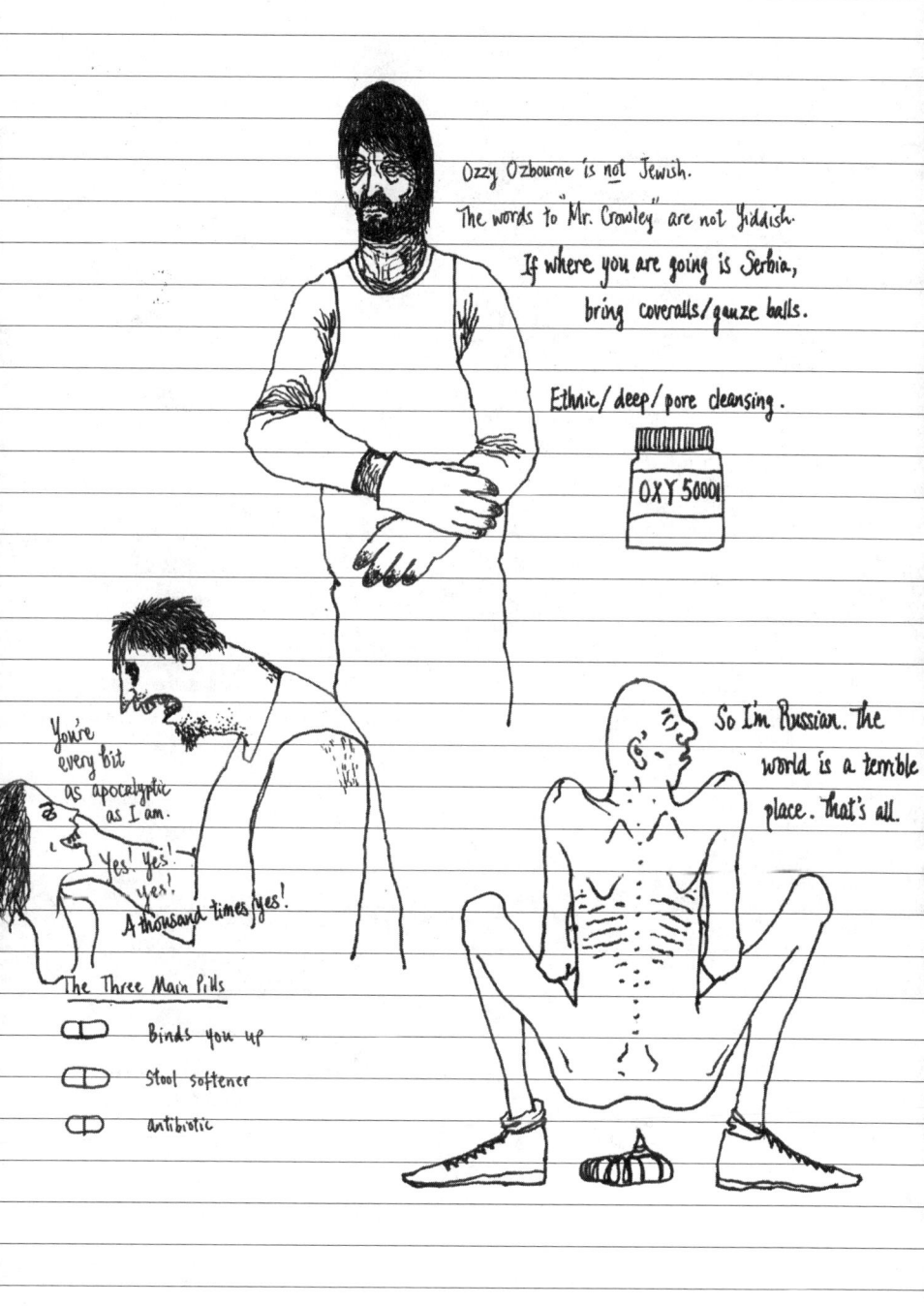

Bemis took his own life — for a reason that has become all-too-familiar: "Snowman's Pass" and "Win a Date with Tad Hamilton" on cable on the same night.

I find comfort in realizing just how tiny I am in the universe.

Sure it felt good to be back in Chuck's arms, but Hannigan wondered about the road not taken...

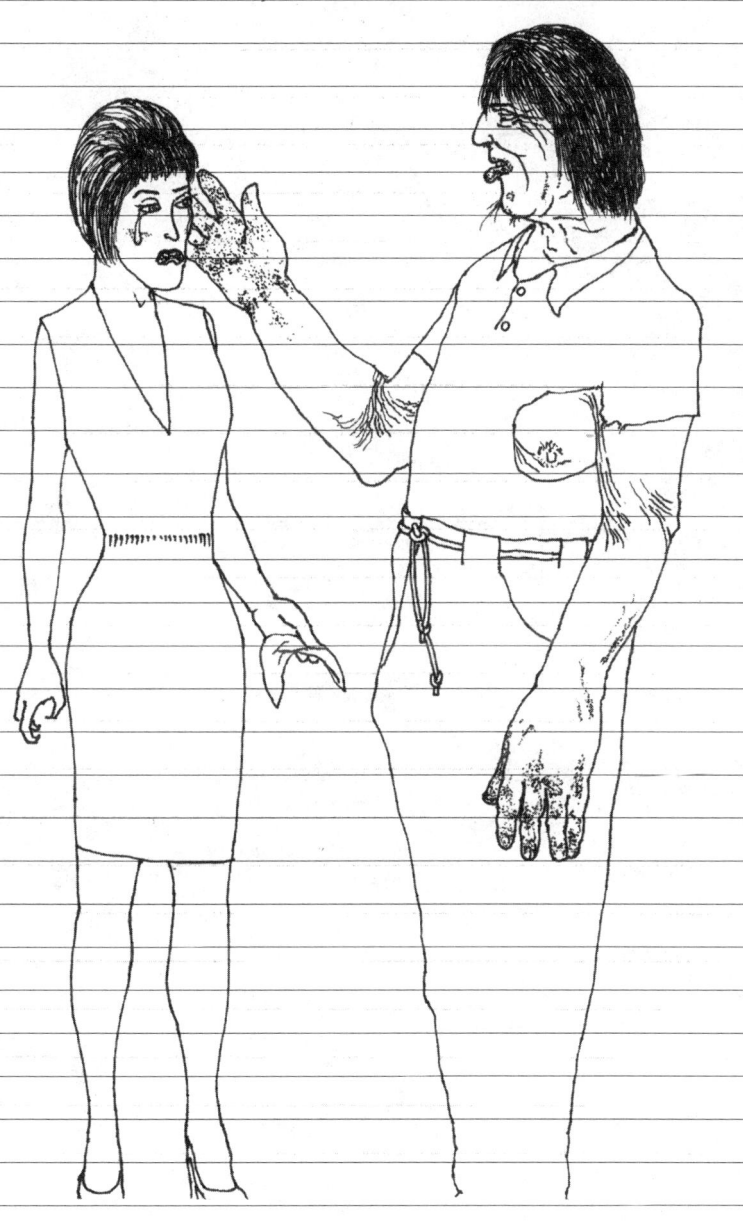

Around the world, Christmas is celebrated in different ways by different people.

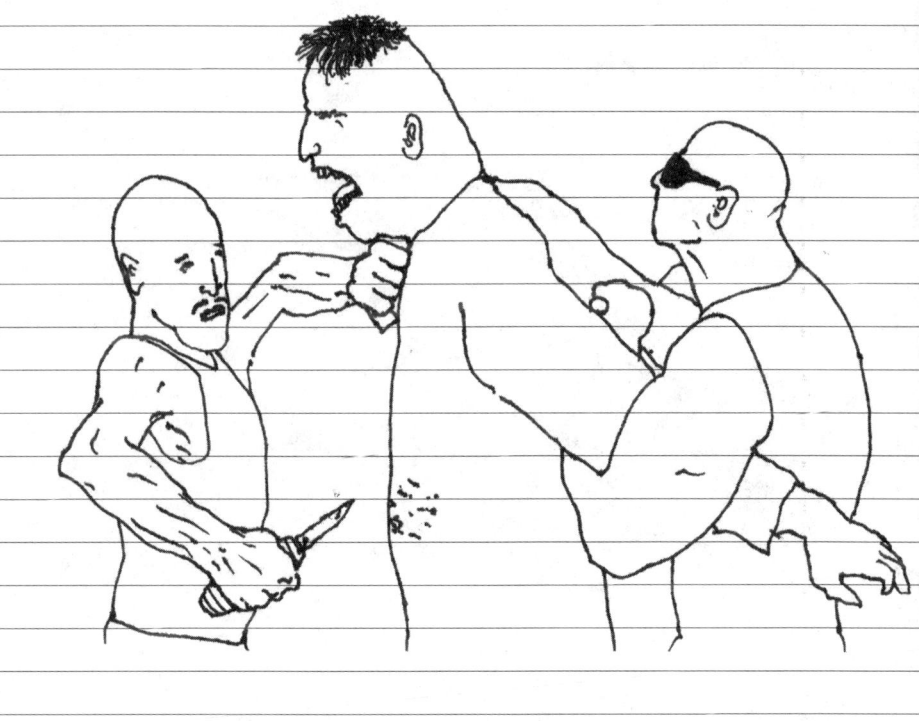

"It's a hymn to Beauty, pendejo!"

"Maybe if you're into ritualized voyeurism, dickhead."

The men down at the Local were always ready to scrap over any misprision, however slight, of Gautier's "Mademoiselle de Maupin".

See how his hair is very freedom and relaxing and so cool. It is very movement. See how he have leather wristbracelet very cool and leather necklace. He have shirt so red. See the shirt have black here, here and there make more cool and freedom. Pants blue. See he wear the shoes relaxing to body and mind. Young people today, go to party, go to dancing, are wear freedom, very movement, very myself, very cool.

年青男孩的造形策略

TEARS OF THE BUN

"They're eating all the pastry...
...it's what they do!"

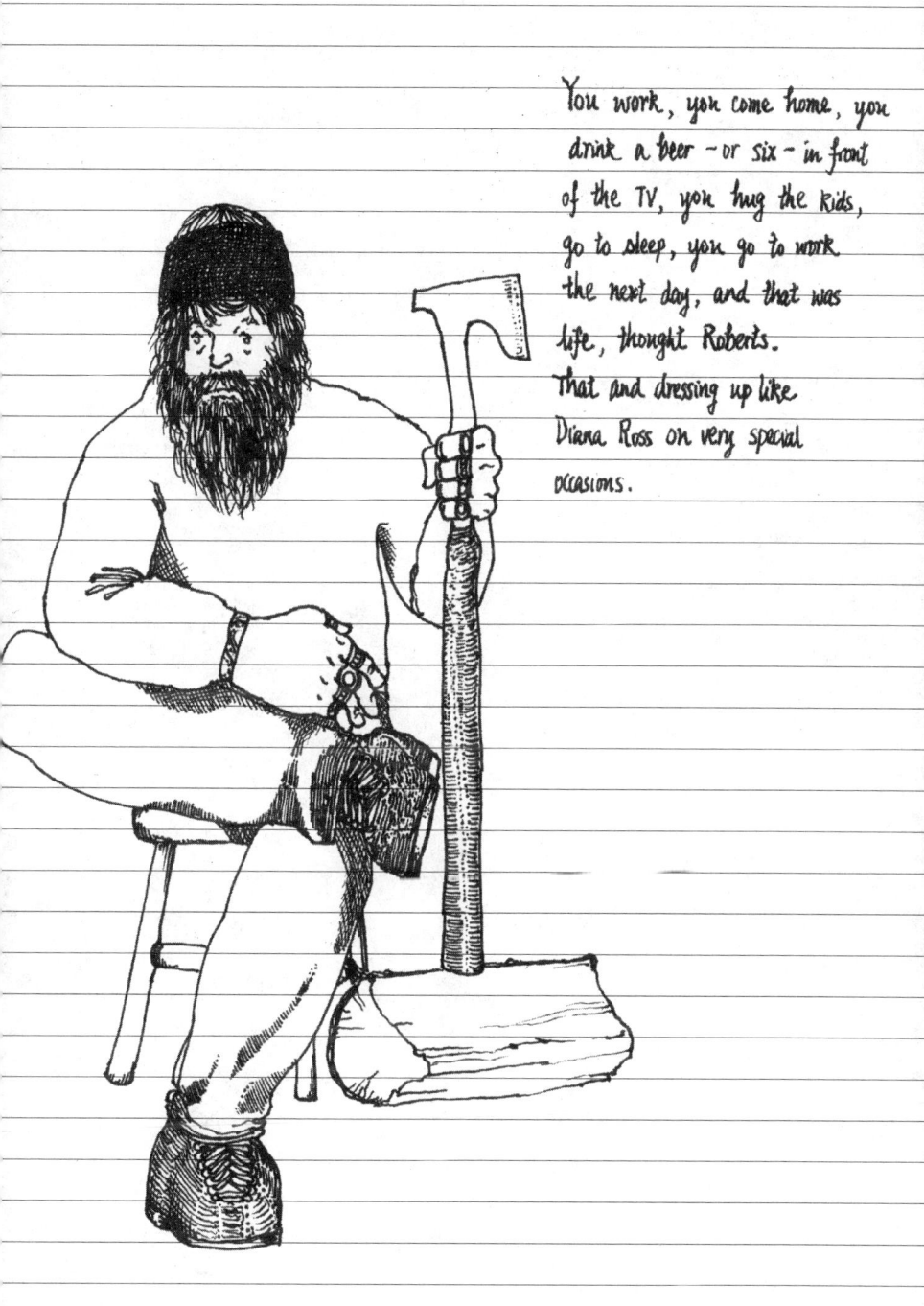

You work, you come home, you drink a beer – or six – in front of the TV, you hug the kids, go to sleep, you go to work the next day, and that was life, thought Roberts. That and dressing up like Diana Ross on very special occasions.

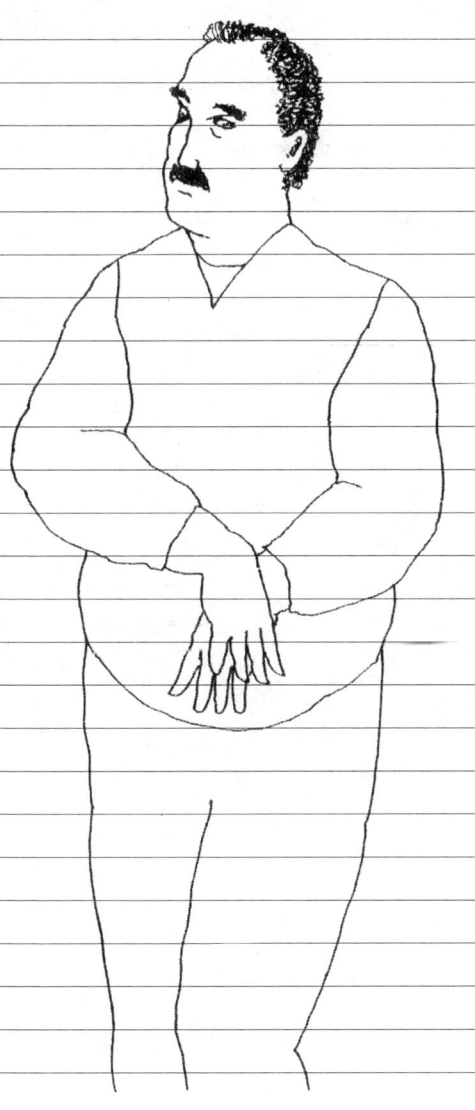

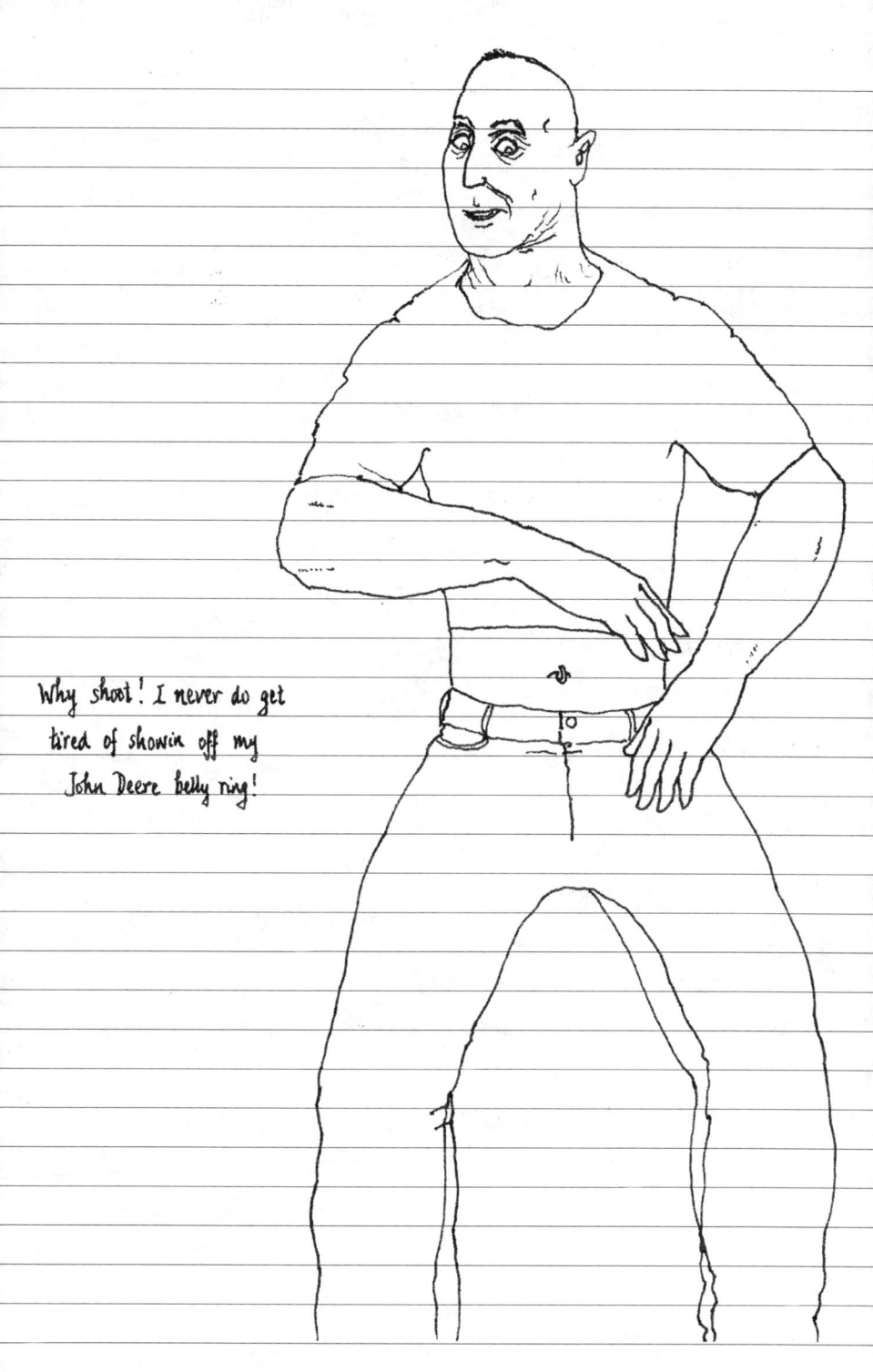

Not the face! Not the face!

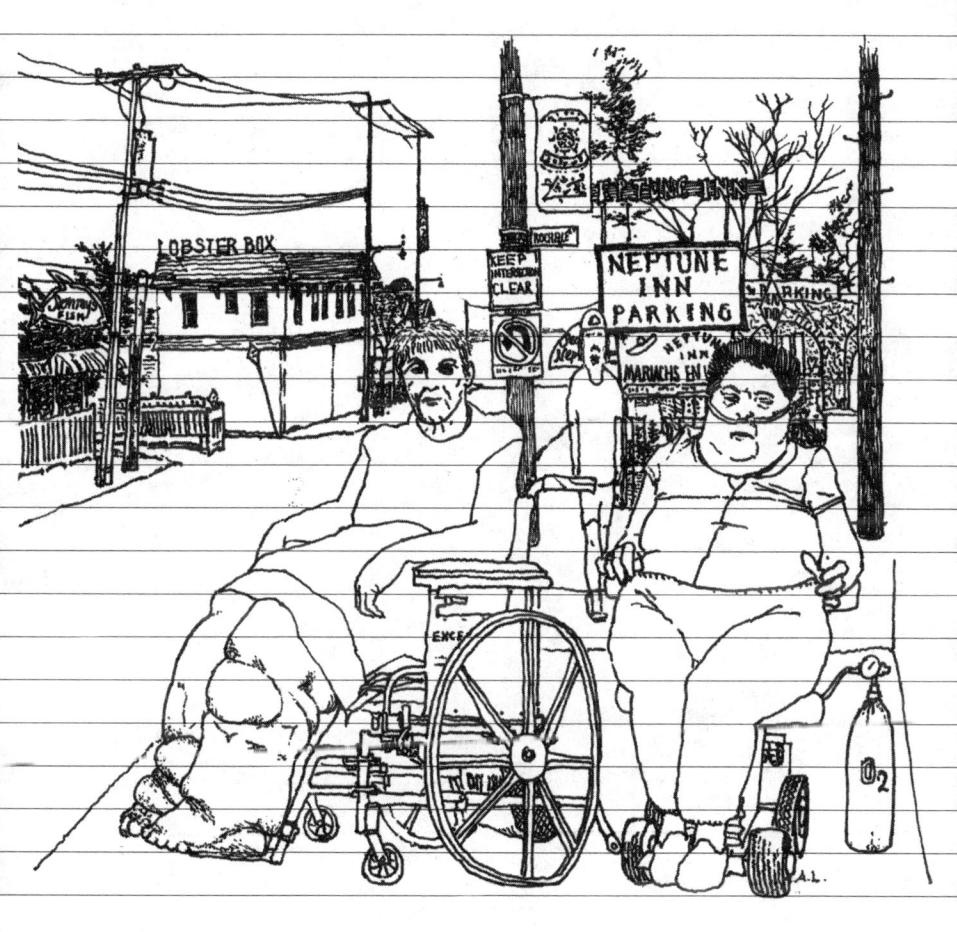

City Island is a close-knit community.

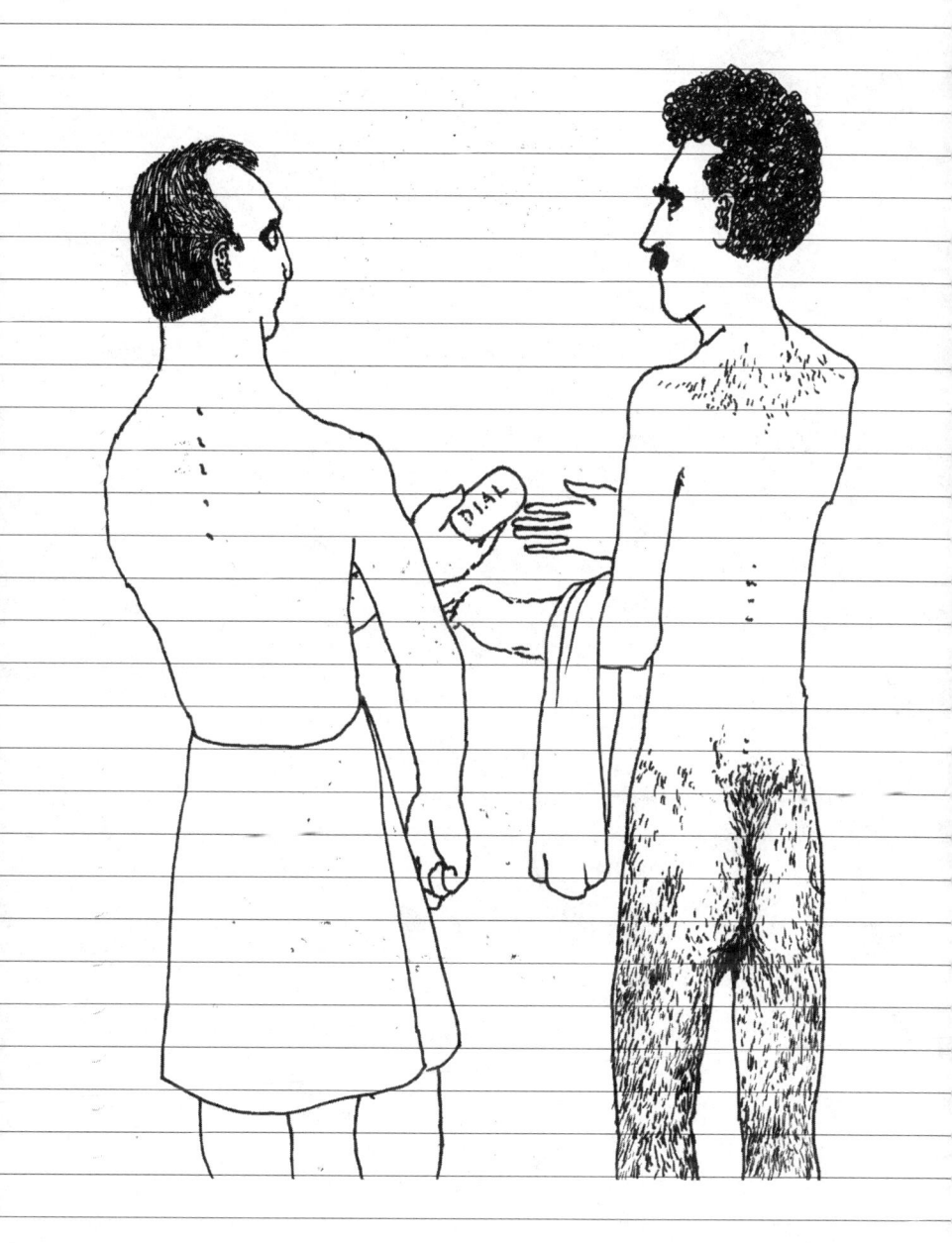

He lead a clean life, I'm telling you. He live clean.
That's his philosophy. Part Indian. More than half.
He don't drink no beer. Only water, juice, fruit juice.
He on a diet. I'm the one seen him do it. He have his body to think of.

Macedonian woman transfixed by "Friday Night Lights."

In line at the Olive Garden,
thinking about what to eat.
How bout the bulionese - however
you say that. Can
you imagine
what my balls
are going to smell like?
What? With the garlic?
The garlic, the cheese,
everything.
My balls are
gonna smell like
a Papa John's.
Why would they
switch franchises?

"I'm a total creature of habit. I always get the same thing here — decaf, non-fat, organic chum."

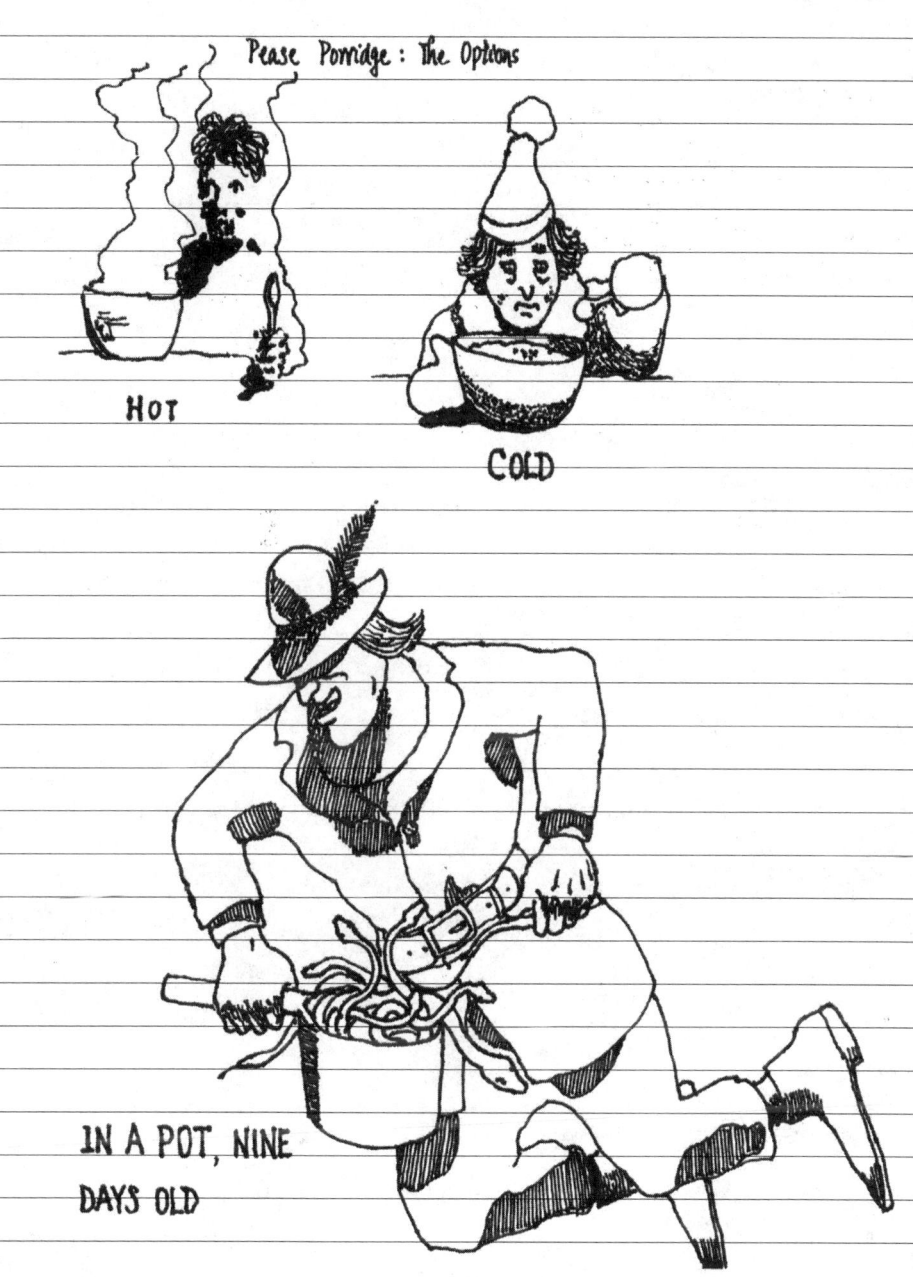

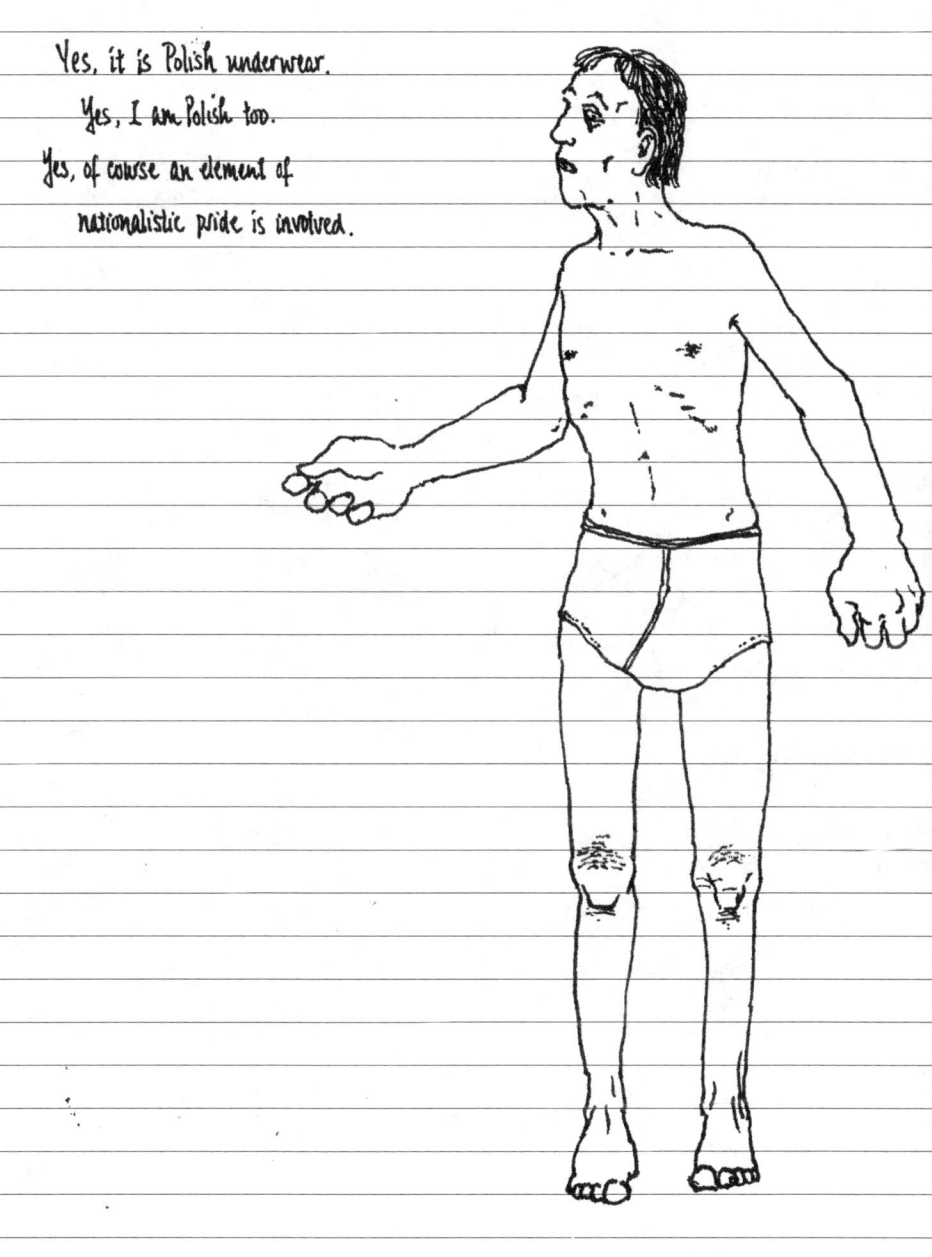

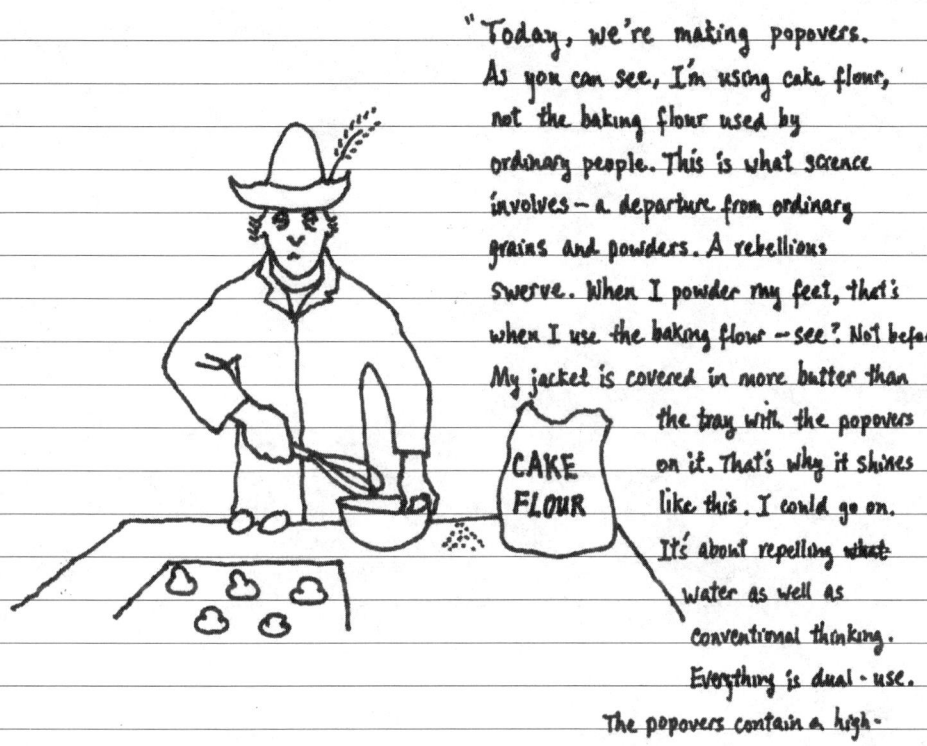

"Today, we're making popovers. As you can see, I'm using cake flour, not the baking flour used by ordinary people. This is what science involves — a departure from ordinary grains and powders. A rebellious swerve. When I powder my feet, that's when I use the baking flour — see? Not before. My jacket is covered in more butter than the tray with the popovers on it. That's why it shines like this. I could go on. It's about repelling water as well as conventional thinking. Everything is dual-use. The popovers contain a high-explosive core. You don't get this on the normal cooking shows. You want to know about the feather? Don't ask! The feather is so I can be identified by friendly forces. The kicker is: there are no friendly forces. I'm alone out here, unfettered. That's the paradox of a feather. Let me get back to baking. So this is what we do: whisk-whisk-whisk, we knead, press, form, we form the popover, it goes on the tray — this is all familiar. What's unfamiliar is — when it's time to bake, you slide yourself into the oven with the tray. That's what no one expects."

我们的婚事…
店堂门市
祝福我吧

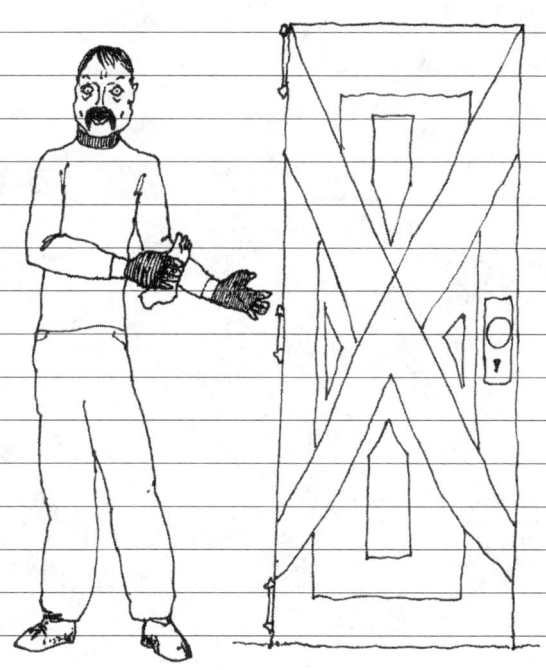

"Perhaps you will follow me downstairs to my workroom where I have many more such treasures and we could look at them together," Vincent breathed.

White Castle has been the ruin of many a man. Outdrink Mike. Do-da, do-da. No vegetables or fruits. Fruits regulate your body temperature. My father used a different social security number for certain things. The Danish and the Japs own the whole thing. And I'm a detective — go figure that shit. You ever buy a new car? Let me see you say that in front of your wife. That's what I tell my honey. I taught him that. I taught him that.

My tour is either Saturday - Sunday or Sunday - Monday. I made it Saturday - Sunday. You would think I would be more concerned with the Bears game. J · E · T · S I'm gonna leave this job early and get to the other job late. Lima beans, kiwis, cantelopes. At least I was able to take the salt away. Stoli Orange. Put it in your tail, Pat.

Showerhead by William Sonoma

What do you want me to say, Moishe? That it was the best ever? Because I'm not going to say that. It was average. Be happy with that.

Food scientist discovers the source of butter taste in deLish ® brand crackers.

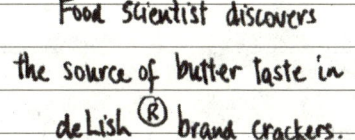

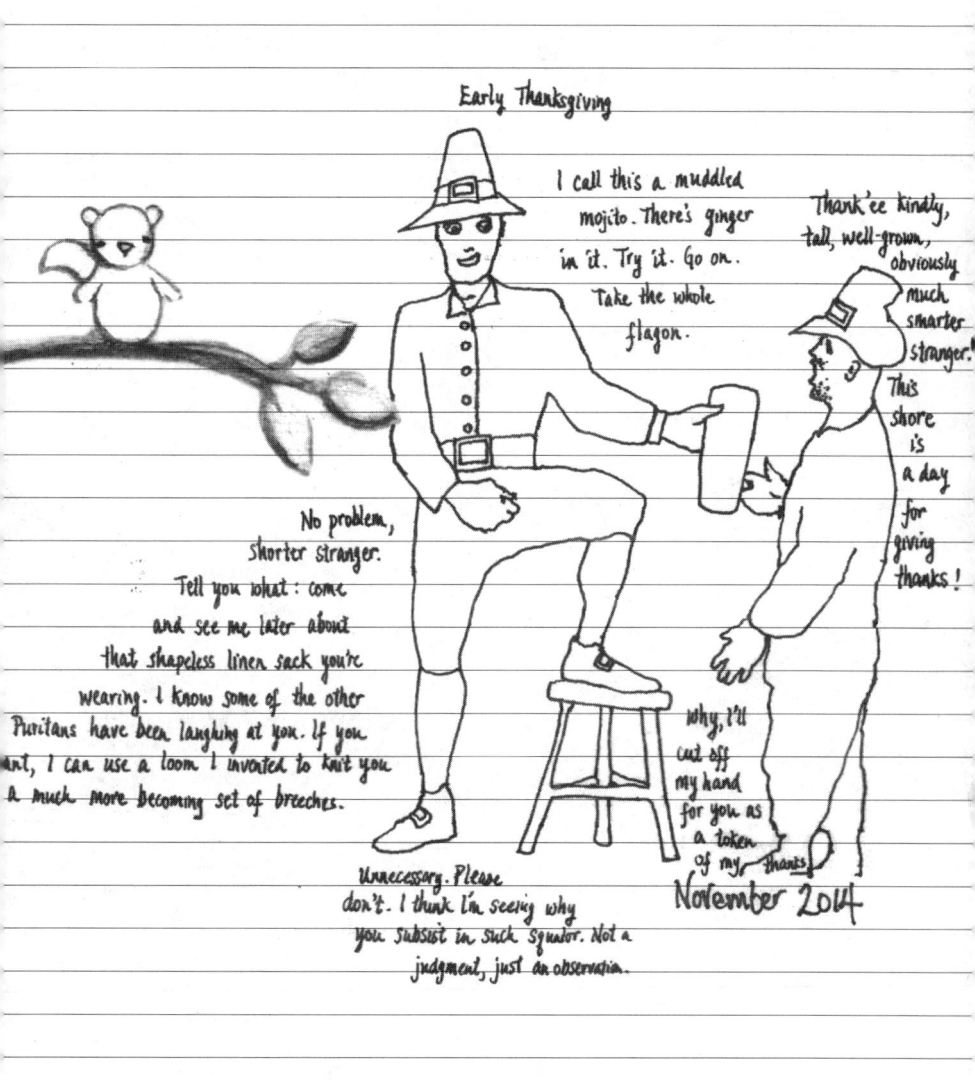

Thus I begin another day dedicated to quality before quantity.

Professor Jenkins, I just wanted you to know: during your lecture series, when you got to the part about ontological historiocity, I experienced a spasm in my anus.

Their lovemaking was hampered by mutual drymouth.